THE LAND OF MUTANTS

AN EROTIC FAIRYTALE

CLOVER'S FANTASY ADVENTURES
BOOK 10

VICTORIA RUSH

VOLUME 10

CLOVER'S FANTASY ADVENTURES -
BOOK 10

COPYRIGHT

The Land of Mutants © 2023 Victoria Rush

Cover Design © 2023 PhotoMaras

ALSO BY VICTORIA RUSH

Adult Fairytales:

The Enchanted Forest: An Erotic Fairytale

The Land of Giants: An Erotic Fairytale

The Dragon's Lair: An Erotic Fairytale

Witch's Brew: An Erotic Fairytale

The Mage's Spell: An Erotic Fairytale

The Mermaid Lagoon: An Erotic Fairytale

The Coven: An Erotic Fairytale

Rapunzel: An Erotic Fairytale

The Seven Dwarfs: An Erotic Fairytale

The Land of Mutants: An Erotic Fairytale

The Erotic Temple: A Sexy Fairytale (Coming Soon)

Erotica Themed Bundles:

Voyeur: Lesbian Erotica Bundle

Public Affairs: A Lesbian Anthology

Futa Fantasies: The Ladyboy Collection

Threesomes: The Lesbian Collection

Threesomes - Volume 2: The Lesbian Collection

First Time: A Lesbian Anthology

Hedonism: An Erotic Anthology

Switch Hitters: Bisexual Erotica

Taboo Erotica: The Lesbian Series

BDSM: The Lesbian Collection

Party Games: The Erotic Collection

Party Games 2: The Erotic Collection

All Girl 1: Lesbian Erotica Bundle

All Girl 2: Lesbian Erotica Bundle

All Girl 3: Lesbian Erotica Bundle

All Girl 4: Lesbian Erotica Bundle

Erotic Fairytale Bundles:

Clover's Fantasy Adventures: Books 1 - 5

Clover's Fantasy Adventures: Books 6 - 10

Erotic Fantasy:

Pirate's Bounty: A Time Travel Adventure

Wild West: A Time Travel Adventure

Private Riley: A Time Travel Adventure

Cleopatra's Secret: A Time Travel Adventure

Bounty Hunter 2125: A Time Travel Adventure

Ninja Assassin: A Time Travel Adventure

The 300: A Time Travel Adventure

Arabian Nights: An Erotic Fairytale (coming soon...)

Steamy Time Travel Bundles:

Riley's Time Travel Adventures: Books 1 - 5

Lesbian Erotica:

The Dinner Party: Lesbian Voyeur Erotica

The Darkroom: Bisexual Voyeur Erotica

Naked Yoga: Lesbian Transgender Erotica

Nude Cruise: Bisexual Voyeur Erotica

Rush Hour: Taboo Public Sex

The Girl Next Door: First Time Lesbian Erotic Romance

Girls' Camp: Lesbian Group Sex

Wet Dream: Ladyboy Fantasy Erotica

The Convent: Taboo Sex with a Nun

Sex Robot: A Dream Sex Machine

The Personal Trainer: Getting Pumped at the Gym

The Dominatrix: BDSM Lesbian Domination

Webcam Chat: Lesbian Online Sex

Paint Me: A Kinky Bodypainting Workshop

The Toy Party: Girls Sharing Sex Toys

The Costume Party: Strapping One On

Swedish Sauna: Lesbian Group Sex

The Therapist: Taboo Lesbian Erotica

Elevator Shaft: Bisexual Threesomes Erotica

Ladyboy: Lesbian Transgender Erotica

Peep Show: Lesbian Voyeur Erotica

The Dare: Public Sex Erotica

Maid Service: Lesbian Threesomes Erotica

The Hitchhiker: First Time Lesbian Erotica

The Housesitter: Spycam Lesbian Erotica

The Spa: Lesbian Group Orgy

Parlor Games: Blindfold Sex Party

The Exchange Student: First Time Lesbian Erotica

The Hostel: Bisexual Group Erotica

The Harem: Lesbian Erotic Romance

The Orient Express: Lesbian Voyeur Erotica

The First Lady: A Forbidden Lesbian Erotic Romance

The Slave: Lesbian BDSM Erotica

The Masseuse: Lesbian Sensuous Erotica

Too Close for Comfort: Lesbian Forbidden Erotica

Naked Twister: A Wild Party Game

Lexi: The Sex App (Lesbian Fantasy Erotica)

Call Girl: Lesbian Bisexual Threesomes Erotica

Circle Jill: Lesbian Masturbation Workshop

The Viewing Room: Masturbation Voyeur Erotica

Spin the Bottle: A Kinky Party Game

The Hair Salon: Lesbian Voyeur Erotica

Tribadism 1: Girls Only Sex Workshop

Tribadism 2: The Art of Scissoring

Tribadism 3: Threeway Hookups

The Kiss: A Game of Oral Sex

Pledge Week: Sorority Sisters

Carny Games 1: A Wild Sex Party

Carny Games 2: A Kinky Sex Party

Carny Games 3: An Erotic Sex Party

Dreamscape: An Artificial Reality Game

Glory Hole: Guess Who's On the Other Side

Joy Ride: A Late Night Erotic Bus Trip

The Blind Girl: An Erotic Romance(Coming Soon)

Lesbian Erotica Bundles:

Jade's Erotic Adventures: Books 1 - 5

Jade's Erotic Adventures: Books 6 - 10

Jade's Erotic Adventures: Books 11 - 15

Jade's Erotic Adventures: Books 16 - 20

Jade's Erotic Adventures: Books 21 - 25

Jade's Erotic Adventures: Books 26 - 30

Jade's Erotic Adventures: Books 31 - 35

Jade's Erotic Adventures: Books 36 - 40

Jade's Erotic Adventures: Books 41 - 45

Jade's Erotic Adventures: Books 46 - 50

Fifty Shades of Jade: Superbundle

Standalone Stories:

The Polynesian Girl: A Lesbian EroticRomance

For the uninhibited...

WANT TO AMP UP YOUR SEX LIFE?

Sign up for my newsletter to receive more free books and other steamy stuff. Discover a hundred different ways to wet your whistle!

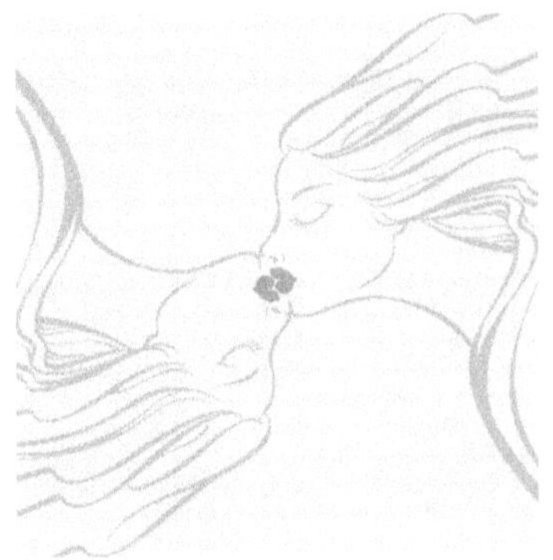

Victoria Rush Erotica

1

After Clover, Tara, and Jessop left their newly liberated dwarf friends, they continued traveling southward, foraging and enjoying the peaceful solitude of the inland forest. But the further they traveled, the fewer settlements they came upon, until they emerged at the base of a large waterfall with some scattered thatch-roof huts and strange-looking people kneeling by the bank of a river. At first, the three friends thought they were washing clothes or collecting water, but the closer they looked through the dense brush, the more their eyes widened in surprise.

The women, having otherwise beautiful, curvy bodies, had three breasts and strange, glistening slits on their stomachs that flared open whenever they bent over the water. And the men, buff and muscular with carved pecs and abs, sported two cocks hanging between their muscular thighs in varying degrees of tumescence. Some of the men were paired up with two women bobbing side-by-side on their elongated organs, while the other women rubbed their bodies together in obvious sexual arousal while their bulbous breasts with thick, hard nipples slid over their partners' abdominal openings with a loud slurping sound.

"Holy shit!" Jessop whispered, holding one of the branches aside with a trembling hand. "Who *are* those people, and what the fuck are they doing?"

"It looks like they're having sex," Clover said.

"That's not the way *I've* seen anybody have sex before," Tara said, shaking her head with a wrinkled brow.

"It seems that they've got some unusual anatomy," Clover nodded, glancing at the women's strange breasts and the men's bifurcated cocks.

"I'll say," Jessop said, shifting uncomfortably behind the bushes while his dick swelled in his pants as he watched the spectacle on the riverbank. "Three tits and multiple cocks? What do they *do* with all those extra appendages?"

"Isn't it *obvious*?" Clover chuckled. "They make use of them in much the same way we do."

"Except they've got a lot more to work with," Tara nodded. "If I had two dicks and three pussies, I'd be using them as often as I could, too."

"Look," Jessop said, pointing to a lone figure further down the riverbank who was humping the opening in her stomach with her curved dick while her three tits bounced on her chest. "There's one with both male *and* female body parts! Where did these people come from?"

"I don't know," Clover said, glancing around the settlement, noticing some farm animals penned behind rough-hewn fences and lush gardens filled with leafy vegetables. "But they seem to be fairly self-sufficient."

"In more ways than one," Tara said, watching the hermaphrodite grunting in pleasure while she played with her nipples and her long appendage pumped in and out of her stomach.

"Maybe we should *introduce* ourselves..." Jessop said, reaching into his pants to straighten out his hardening tool.

"I'd hate to interrupt their obvious pleasure," Clover said. "Although it looks like you're more than willing to barge in on the festivities."

"I think another *dick* is the last thing they need right now," Tara chuckled.

Suddenly, the three friends heard some rustling in the bushes behind them, and they turned around to see a group of naked men lined up, pointing spears toward them. Tara instinctively reached for her bow hanging over her back, but Clover placed her hand on her arm, motioning for her to stand down.

"Let's not stir things up any more than we need to," she said, raising her hands over her head to show the trio meant no harm to the strange band of natives.

The tribesmen paused for a moment then one of them stepped forward, thrusting his spear angrily in their direction.

"What are you *doing* here?" he said.

"Nothing," Clover said. "We just stumbled upon your settlement. We didn't mean to interfere in your...*activities*."

"You're *humans*," he grunted. "Nothing ever good comes from mingling with your kind."

"I understand," Clover said, remembering how their dwarf friends had been banished from the local village and persecuted for their unusual features. "We'll just continue on our way and give you no trouble–"

"Wait," Tara said, pulling Clover back down beside her. "They've got a lot more food than we do. Maybe we could offer a *trade* in order to stock up on provisions before we move on..."

The lead tribesman paused as he ran his eyes over Tara's diminutive figure, squinting at her pointed ears.

"What could you humans possibly offer us?" he said.

"Well, technically, I'm an *elf*," she said, peering down at the tribesman's twin phalluses bumping together between his legs. "I'm not built like other humans, much like you. Plus, we're pretty handy with our tools. We might be able to help you capture some wild game like boar, grouse, and rabbits."

"We already have plenty of chickens and goats–"

One of the other tribesmen glanced at Tara's firm tits covered by her animal-skin bodysuit and gently lowered the angry tribesman's spear.

"They seem harmless enough," he said. "Why don't we introduce them to *Akirie* and see what she says? Maybe they can prove useful to us..."

"Humfft!" the lead tribesman huffed, pulling back his spear and thumping the blunt end on the ground. "Come, we'll see what our leader wants to do with you. But keep your weapons sheathed, lest we poke you with our lances."

"I might kind of like that," Tara grinned, noticing the pronged cocks of the second tribesman beginning to swell as he ogled her sexy figure.

When the trio emerged from the brush with the group of tribesman escorting them toward the central courtyard, the rest of the tribespeople stopped what they were doing and peered up at the strange intruders while they decoupled, displaying their glistening sex organs.

"Holy fuck," Tara grunted as she passed one of the men with his erect organs pointing at forty-five degree opposite angles over his ripped abdomen. "Can you imagine what we could do with two of those?"

"I'm beginning to wonder," Clover nodded as her eyes flared at his throbbing equipment.

"I'm starting to feel a bit *inadequate* around here," Jessop sighed, staring at the tribesmen's huge, swelling tools.

"Don't worry, Jessop," Tara said, noticing his dick angling upward in his tight pants while he stared at the women's triple tits. "If you play your cards right, you might be able to show these natives a few tricks of your own."

"Oh, I've got a few tricks up my sleeve, alright," he smiled, walking past a young tribesman jerking both of his erect poles with two hands inside one of the thatched huts. "I just don't know where to start."

2

As the group approached the center of the courtyard, they noticed an elderly woman squatting next to a small campfire, grinding some grains in a stone bowl while some of the younger tribeswoman chopped vegetables and stirred a pot hanging over the flame. The woman had three breasts like the others, though hers were sagging a bit more, and the slits on her abdomen were framed with thin tendrils of gray hair. When the women saw us approaching under escort from the armed tribesmen, they paused what they were doing, peering up at us curiously.

"Who are these strange people you bring from the forest, Elyon?" the elderly woman said, peering at the first tribesman with a furrowed brow.

"They said they're drifters," the tribesman said.

The woman paused, darting her eyes over the three friends' figures, then she glanced at Clover, who was at the front of the pack.

"What is your purpose, infringing upon our space?" she said.

"We meant no harm or disrespect," Clover said. "We were simply foraging for food and stumbled upon your settlement."

"Is that what you need those strange *weapons* for?" she said, noticing Tara's bow and Jessop's sword.

"Mostly," Clover nodded. "Though we also use them to defend ourselves, when necessary."

"You must have traveled a long way," the woman nodded, squinting at Clover's and Tara's breasts, wrapped in their tight-fitting, animal-skin bodysuits. "There are no humans in these parts."

"Yes," Clover said. "We thought we might find more wild game closer to the mountains. We're quite hungry after our long trek."

The woman paused again, noticing how the two groups were staring at each other's bodies, seemingly more interested in amorous discourse than matters of war.

"They said they were looking for boar and grouse," the second tribesman said, stepping forward.

"Those are difficult to catch," the old woman said. "They'd make a welcome addition to our stew."

"Hard to catch with *spears* maybe," Tara smiled, glancing up at the second tribesman. "But not so difficult with a bow and arrow."

"Perhaps you can demonstrate your skill after sharing lunch with us," the woman nodded. "A roast boar would be a perfect centerpiece for our planned festival tonight..."

"Oh?" Jessop said, having a hard time keeping his eyes from straying below the women's faces onto their bobbing breasts and strange row of slits running up the front of their bare abdomens. "Were you planning some kind of celebration?"

"It's our monthly *fertility festival*," the woman nodded.

"Marking the emergence of the new moon. We all sit around the fire watching our younger members mating, to encourage the propagation of our species. Would you like to join us in the celebration?"

"Um, sure," Jessop grinned, crossing his hands over his crotch to conceal his swelling erection in his pants.

"Come join us in the circle and make yourselves comfortable," the woman said, motioning for the tribesmen to sit down next to the visitors.

"Do you mind my asking how you came to populate this settlement?" Clover asked, peering at the tribespeople's strange appendages. "We've never seen people with your unique...*features*."

"It started when one female was born with two *cavas*," the woman said. "Her community tried to eliminate her when she came of age, and she escaped to the forest with her young lover to start a new life away from the humans. Their offspring were also born with unusual anomalies, and before long, an entire settlement of gifteds formed next to this beautiful waterfall."

"Is that what you call your people?" Clover said, smiling at the old lady.

"Yes," she said. "The humans call us freaks or mutants, but we prefer to look at our special endowments as a gift from the gods."

"I can see why," Tara nodded, feeling her bodysuit moistening between her legs while she peered at the semi-tumescent, pronged cocks of the tribesmen squatting around the fire.

"But why *two* cocks?" Clover said, reflecting back on her evolutionary biology class from high school. "Normally, evolution selects those features that are most suited for the survival of any particular species..."

"Why *not*?" Elyon said. "We have two hands, two eyes, and two ears. The more reproductive organs we have, the greater our chance of producing offspring."

"Our fertility rate is lower than most humans," the elderly woman nodded. "Having two lingum and multiple cava helps ensure enough seeds are planted to produce a new cohort."

"Why three *breasts* then?" Tara said, squinting at the young tribeswomen's long nipples protruding from their firm orbs.

"We have fewer live births," the old lady said. "But larger *broods* when there is a successful reproduction. The extra milka ensures we have enough food to sustain the children until they're able to feed themselves."

"Makes sense," Jessop nodded, trying to conceal his angled erection in his trousers while he sat cross-legged in front of the fire, ogling the beautiful women with their strange abdominal cavities dripping as they stared between his legs. "But why do the men have two cocks and the women have more cava?"

"The more cava, the more opportunities there are for joining our sexual appendages," the woman said. "Unlike *human* pair-bonding, where one woman normally joins with one man for life to raise their young, in our society we encourage as much cross-pollination as possible to maximize our fertility rate and share in the child-rearing together as a community."

"That sounds amazing," Clover said, enjoying the pungent soup as she took another sip of the delicious stew. "I can see now why you call yourselves *gifted*. It sounds like a truly egalitarian society where everyone loves and supports one another."

"It's worked for us so far," the old woman nodded. "At

least, without the interference of the outside world. We're very protective of our community and our unique genetic makeup."

"So you've never experimented with *interspecies* mating between humans and your kind?" Tara said.

"Not so far," she said, noticing one of the tribesman's pronged cocks dripping a trail of dew over his throbbing crowns. "But judging by the way Arel's been staring at you ever since you came into our camp, I'm not sure how much longer I'll be able to keep you separated."

"Perhaps you don't need to," Tara grinned. "He can help me forage for boar in the woods and I can use *my* unique talents to land a different type of game."

"That's fine by me, assuming Arel's willing. Perhaps your friends would like to join in the mating activities during our festival later tonight?"

"We might be persuaded..." Clover smiled, eyeing up one of the tribesman who was openly stroking his upturned cocks with both hands while he stared at her.

"I'm *definitely* in," Jessop nodded, grinning at the pretty maidens while they gently caressed their glistening slits.

3

W hen they finished their soup, Tara and Arel excused themselves from the group, disappearing into the forest to begin foraging for food for the evening's dinner. But as they began scanning the landscape, they kept peering at each other's unusual figures, obviously distracted by other motivations besides hunting.

"How do you want to do this, exactly?" Arel said, darting his eyes over her upturned breasts and the camel-toe outline in her tight bodysuit. "I mean, the searching for *boar*–"

"The hard part is finding them," Tara said, glancing upward to watch a buzzard circling over the brush a few hundred yards away. "Why don't you keep a lookout on that hillock next to the clearing? The buzzard probably means there's carrion nearby. If there are any boar in the area, the scent will soon attract them."

"Okay," Arel said, disappointed he couldn't stay closer to the pretty elf while they foraged for game. "But yell if you need me. I'm pretty handy with my spear."

"I bet you are," Tara grinned, glancing down at his bobbing cocks. "I'm sure I'll be able to use your special talents soon enough."

"Good," Arel nodded. "I'll point my spear in the direction of the animal if I see anything."

"Perfect," Tara said. "Then run toward me to drive it toward my position. I'll take care of the rest."

"Will do," Arel said, trotting off toward the ridge while Tara ogled his muscular ass and bouncing pricks between his legs.

"Damn," she muttered to herself, feeling her pussy throbbing in her tight bodysuit. "I hope I can aim true when the time comes, with these trembling hands. I'd rather be using them for something else right now."

She headed over in the direction of the circling buzzard then glanced up at Arel standing on the hill with his legs spread apart.

"Fuck, that's a fine specimen," she grunted, soaking up his athletic figure and oversized genitals while she felt herself breathing harder.

Suddenly, Arel began shaking his spear in the air, then he tilted it downward with two hands, pointing it a few yards to her left. She saw a dark patch of fur scurrying into the clearing, then she took up the chase, trying to get a closer bead on the boar. At the same time, Arel began running in the opposite direction, darting and weaving through the brush in the direction of the snorting and squealing animal. But when he cornered it on the other side of the clearing, the boar lowered its head and charged toward him. Just as Tara emerged into the clearing, the boar rammed his horns into Arel's hips, toppling him over his head.

"Arel!" Tara shouted, running toward the fallen

tribesman while she pulled an arrow out of her quiver and hurtled an arrow toward the boar's flanks, spearing it through its heart.

When the animal dropped onto the ground next to Arel, Tara skidded onto her knees beside him, holding his head in his hands.

"Are you alright?" she said. "Did the animal *injure* you?"

"It's nothing serious," he said, trying to rise up on his knees.

"You've been cut!" Tara said, noticing a nasty gash on the inside of his thighs.

"It's fine," Arel said. "I've had worse scrapes before–"

"We should get that covered to stem the bleeding," she nodded, placing her bow and quiver on the ground and tearing a patch of loincloth off the front of her bodysuit.

While she wrapped the strip of cloth around Arel's upper thigh, his cocks twitched as he glanced down at her bare abdomen, peering at her flexing abdomen.

"Thanks," he said, appraising her makeshift tourniquet. "It looks like the swelling has stopped. But I'm not so sure about the *rest* of me..."

"Let me take a closer look," Tara smiled, pushing him back onto the ground and spreading his legs apart.

She gripped each of his prongs with her fingertips, then lifted them up gently to inspect the underside of his throbbing instruments and his human-looking balls, nodding assuredly.

"Looks like everything's in working order," she grinned, running her hand softly down the inside of his V-shaped crease and over his tightening testicles. "It seems that you'll still be able to make plenty more gifted babies."

"Maybe I don't *want* to make any more gifted babies

right now," he said, sitting up and cradling Tara's chin in his hands. "I'd prefer to make more *human* babies..."

"I'm not quite sure how that would work," Tara said, drifting her face closer to his as they peered into each other's eyes. "But I'm willing to give it a try if you are."

Arel pressed his lips against Tara's, then the elf tore off her bodysuit while they lashed their tongues together. When she exposed her naked body to him, he peered between her legs at her dripping pussy with a puzzled expression, unsure what to do next.

"I'm not used to women having their cavas between their *legs*," he said. "I'm not sure how we should do this exactly–"

"It probably works pretty much the same way as you're used to," Tara chuckled, spreading her legs apart and climbing on top of him in an angled position. "You put the male part into the female part and move it all about."

"Just *one*?" Arel said, staring at her glistening, pink vulva.

"For now," Tara nodded, grabbing the tip of one of his shafts and pointing it toward her slit. "Maybe I can keep the other one busy some other way..."

When she lowered herself over his throbbing organ, they both moaned, then Tara grasped his other dick pressed off to the side with both hands, stroking it up and down while she rocked her hips over his embedded tool.

"Unghh," he grunted, staring at Tara with wide eyes. "I've never done it this way before–"

"You mean you've never had a *hand job*?" she huffed, grinding her hips into the base of his joined organs.

"Not with another *woman*," he nodded. "Akirie says we should always save our precious seeds for our partners."

"Do you *like* it?" Tara smiled, twisting her fingers over his swelling glans while she fondled his balls with her other hand.

"Yes," he groaned. "You're stimulating me in ways that a *cava* can't. I've done it by myself of course, but it's infinitely better when somebody *else* is doing it."

"That's not the *only* way I can stimulate it. After I get off, I want to lick your pricks with my *mouth*..."

"Do you want to get off now?" he said, straightening his arms, attempting to pull his hips away from her pumping pussy.

"No, I meant *get off* in a different way–to *climax* first. I'm not done with you yet."

"Okay, don't stop," Arel groaned while his pupils began to dilate. "I'm going to sperm soon. This is arousing me much faster than usual."

"Mmm," Tara smiled when she noticed a stream of liquid beginning to spill out the top of his free cock. "I want to watch you shoot your sperm into my hands while I come over your other cock–er *lingum*. Fuck me hard..."

"Yes," Arel grunted as he humped his hips faster against Tara's dripping slit and squeezing hands. "It's coming now. Here comes my honey–"

Tara had to chuckle at the funny terms the gifted people used to describe their sex organs, but when she felt Arel spurting in her hands and grunting while he jerked his hips against her pussy, she felt her own orgasm soon wash over her, and she gripped his inside shaft with her contracting pussy while she squeezed his other organ with her hands. It was the most unique experience she'd ever had making love to a man, and she savored the feeling of his warm liquid spraying over her tits while she felt him pulsing inside her. When they finally finished shaking and convulsing, she dropped down onto the ground beside him, panting in excitement as she peered into the tribesman's bright blue eyes.

"Did you enjoy that as much as I did?" he panted, rolling his fingers over her cum-soaked breasts. "Did you climax together with me?"

"Yes," Tara smiled. "Although I have a feeling you enjoyed that *twice* as much as I did."

She peered between Arel's legs, noticing his still-erect prongs dripping a stream of semen down the underside of his shafts while they bobbed excitedly over his heaving stomach.

"But something tells me you've still got plenty of honey left in the tank..."

She rolled over and swallowed each of his erections in turn, rolling her tongue around the flared frenulums of his paired heads while she hummed in delight.

"Oh my God," Arel groaned, slamming his head back down onto the grass. "Who needs a *cava* when you've got all these *other* incredible parts to stimulate our organs?"

"I imagine your honey might be needed *elsewhere* once in a while," Tara chuckled, coming up for air as she bobbed her head between each of his throbbing poles. "But let's worry about that a little later..."

4

———

Later that evening, the tribespeople prepared the courtyard for their elaborate celebration, creating a huge circle around the central fire pit, bedecked with garlands of orchid, poppy, and lotus flowers. Then the group placed the boar that Tara and Arel had caught on a spit over the fire, with giant helpings of cucumber, eggplant, and avocado generously apportioned for the spectators arranged around the perimeter. When it finally came time for the ceremony, Akirie sat next to the three friends, with the older tribespeople sitting in an outer circle, and the younger ones in a slightly smaller one closer to the fire.

After everyone was seated, one of the older tribesmen began rhythmically beating a large drum while the others chanted loudly. Then the group in the inner circle stood up and started dancing in a rotating pattern around the garland of flowers, bumping their hips together and shaking their hips, becoming increasingly aroused while the rest of the tribe clapped and chanted in encouragement. It didn't take long for the young men's organs to swell and rise over their stomachs, while the women's slits began to flare open and drip fluid, making their bellies glisten in the reflection of the crackling fire.

"That has to be the *sexiest* belly dance I've ever seen," Clover said, whispering into Tara's ear.

"I'm too busy looking at the *men*," Tara nodded, staring at Arel's bouncing prongs while he skipped around the fire in growing excitement.

"What happened between the two of you out there in the forest this afternoon?" Clover said, glancing at Tara's ripped bodysuit. "You haven't been able to take your eyes off each other since you returned with the captured boar."

"Arel suffered a cut to his leg during the chase, and I had to tend to his wound," Tara smiled.

"Exactly what kind of tending did you do?"

"The kind that required me to get extra close to his twin appendages."

"And was it *twice* as good as usual?"

"I don't see *Arel* complaining," Tara chuckled, watching her paramour glancing at her while he swung his forked erections proudly in her direction. "But I think we're just starting to scratch the surface of possibilities, in a manner of speaking."

"Something tells me we're going to see a few *more* unusual hookups before the night is over," Clover smiled, noticing the dancing tribesmen slapping their organs against the women's hips and the women rubbing their bellies together.

"I hope so," Tara said. "I've been fantasizing about all the ways the men and women can use their equipment all day."

"You're not the *only* one," Jessop said, sitting on the opposite side of Tara, with his erection pressing through the outline of his pants. "Although in *my* case, the only man involved in the fantasy is *me*."

"Are you sure about that?" Tara said, glancing at the lone hermaphrodite dancing between the men and women, swishing her hips as her large, curved instrument slapped against her belly next to her flaring slits. "You don't think you'd like a piece of that cock in the middle of the circle? I know you've got a thing for ladyboys–"

"Possibly," Jessop groaned, caressing his throbbing erection. "But it looks like she's got plenty of *other* outlets for that pretty poker."

Suddenly, a pair of the dancing men and women separated from the group and entered the inner ring, facing one another while they shimmied their bodies together, only a few inches apart. Before long, the man began slapping his erect organs against the side of the woman's belly, creating a row of welts and a trail of pre-cum on her glistening stomach. The woman placed her palms over her stomach and rubbed them in circles, mixing the man's dew with her own juices dribbling down the front of her abdomen.

"I hope that's not the end of their copulation ritual," Clover said, leaning over next to the old woman. "I was kind of hoping to see those body parts mingling in a more *direct* way–"

"Give it time," the woman nodded. "This is just the first part of the courtship dance, intended to stimulate their juices."

"It looks like more like an act of a *war*," Tara said, squinting her eyes as the two partners bounced their bodies together.

But before long, the man and the woman began to slow down the gyrations of their hips, then they moved closer together, pressing the tips of the tribesman's forked cocks next to the two lowest slits on the woman's abdomen. When his organs slipped inside her holes, they pressed their bodies together, wrapping their arms around one another as they rocked their hips in synchronicity with the drums.

"That's pretty *hot*," Clover nodded, beginning to feel the crotch of her bodysuit moistening while she watched the amorous couple fornicating only a few yards away.

She turned toward the old lady again, peering at her with a curious expression.

"Do the women enjoy it as much as the men?" she asked. "I mean, do they have special sensory organs that make it pleasurable, like with human females?"

"Yes," the woman nodded. "Though in our case, our pleasure centers are positioned near the *back* of our cavas, rather than at the opening. I think it's the gods' way of encouraging full insertion, to ensure the man's seed reaches the woman's ovary."

"That's *ingenious*," Tara said. "Though a tad disappointing. It must make it harder for the women to pair up by themselves sometimes to fully enjoy sex..."

"Not as much as you'd think," the old lady smiled. "They've become quite resourceful at using *other* phallic-shaped objects to stimulate themselves. Although we generally discourage this practice, since it reduces the opportunities to procreate the natural way."

"Do you *hear* that, Jessop?" Clover smiled, noticing her friend's hand down his pants, jerking his hard-on while he watched the couple writhing in the circle. "It sounds like the men are encouraged to hook up with the women as often as they can. Just remember to sink your dick *all* the way into their cavas if you have a chance to fuck one of them later tonight."

"I don't think you'll have to worry about that," Jessop

grunted, fapping his dick harder as his face began to flush in rising excitement.

Suddenly, the drummer's beat began to gather momentum, and the pair in the middle of the circle rocked their hips faster to match his tempo. As their buttocks began to clench more tightly, they wrapped their arms around one another's shoulders, angling their faces up toward the moon, gaping their mouths open while they grunted in unison with the crowd's loud chants. After a few more seconds, their bodies began to shake while they emitted a strange growling sound, then they held onto one another until they stopped trembling and the drumbeat slowly receded.

"That was interesting," Tara said, pulling her dripping hand out of her ripped bodysuit. "But it seems strange that there wasn't any *kissing* at any point in the demonstration."

"There's no place for *love* in our culture," the old lady said, glancing down at the three friends' soaked crotches. "The act of sex in our tribe is purely for procreation. The men are discouraged from forming close emotional connections with the women, lest they lose the incentive to spread their seeds as wide as possible. The more intermingling between the males and females, the greater their chances of having successful conception."

"I'd be happy to help out if you need a few extra seeds," Jessop said, still holding his hard-on in his pants.

"You might have to wait a little longer," Clover chuckled, glancing at the couple in the middle of the circle. "I have a feeling these two aren't finished yet..."

The three friends peered back toward the middle of the fire pit, noticing the woman who'd just had sex with the young tribesman kneeling on her knees while the tribesman's partially erect and dripping cocks bobbed in front of her face.

"I thought you said you didn't want any seed going to *waste*?" Clover said, turning toward the old lady with a puzzled expression. "It looks like they're about to have oral sex..."

"We don't outlaw oral coupling if it's intended to arouse the men and stimulate the replenishment of their sperm," the woman said. "This is why the women have three or more cavas. The more receptacles for the men's sperm, the greater the chance one of their ovaries will produce a viable egg."

"It's a pity they don't have two *mouths* also," Tara chuckled while she watched the kneeling woman bobbing her head between the tribesman's swelling dicks, stimulating each of them in turn with expert licking of his two organs.

"Holy fuck," Jessop said, jerking his cock with newfound enthusiasm while he watched the woman swallowing each of her partner's poles. "If that's how the women give head around here, I might be interested in sticking my dick all the way inside something *else* when I get an opportunity."

"You better save your stuff when you get the chance," Tara smiled, noticing streams of pre-cum dripping down the underside of his upturned shaft poking out of his unbuttoned trousers.

"I'm trying," Jessop panted. "But it's getter *harder* by the moment."

After a few more minutes, the kneeling woman lifted her head off the tribesman's now fully erect cocks and straightened out her body, positioning her two upper slits closer to his bouncing organs. The tribesman bent his knees slightly and squatted down a few inches lower, then the woman grasped the tips of his poles and pointed them into her two unused slits. Once again, the drumbeat began to progressively pound louder and faster as the couple rocked their bodies together, this time with the woman licking the front of his flexing abdomen while he humped his hips against her torso.

"Holy shit," Clover said to Tara, sliding her fingers over the front of her dripping bodysuit. "Just when I thought it couldn't get any sexier. I'm afraid these tribesmen are going to find our single pussies pretty uninspiring if we ever get a chance to hook up with them."

"I wouldn't be so sure about that," Tara said, glancing back in the direction of Arel, who was dancing ever more excitedly around the circle in anticipation of his turn in the inner ring. "I can think of *plenty* of ways to keep all of their body parts occupied."

Clover smiled while she watched Tara's hand moving under her bodysuit again, pressing her digits harder against her swelling clit.

"Maybe we can *both* have a turn with one of them when the time comes," she said.

"That's one of the ways I was thinking," Clover moaned.

As the drummer's beat began to escalate again in both volume and tempo, the couple in the middle of the pit rocked their bodies harder together until once again, they angled their heads up to the sky, imploring the gods to smile upon their act of public procreation. When the beat came to a crescendo, they howled again, jerking their bodies together as their slippery abdomens quivered in ecstasy. The sound of the drumbeat and the loud chanting almost drowned out the sound of the three friends groaning along with them while they creamed their uniforms soon after.

The old lady peered over toward them and glanced down at their dripping hands, nodding in approval.

Whether she'd staged their participation in the ceremony purely as *passive* observers, or as more active participants, they couldn't be sure. But one way or the other, one thing was for certain. The trio had never witnessed such as erotic spectacle before, and they were happy enough to watch from the sidelines until they had a turn to fulfill each of their own mutual fantasies.

5

———————

After the couple in the middle of the pit exited the ring, another group of dancing tribespeople entered the circle soon after. But this time it was *two* men and one woman. Tara wasn't sure if she was excited or disappointed that Arel hadn't yet had his turn, eager as she was to see his forked pokers in action again, but hopeful she'd soon have a chance to participate in the action herself. While she watched the men's twin cocks rising to full rigidity as the woman teased them with her three tits, she slid her hand down the front of her tunic again while her friends peered on in a similar state of excitement.

"It looks like that hole in your suit turned out to be fortuitous in more ways than *one*," Clover chuckled as she peered down at her friend jilling herself.

"It's definitely coming in handy," Tara nodded, circling her fingers over her throbbing clit. "Why don't you take your suit off? It's not like anyone's going to care. These native people seem happy to prance around in the buff all day long."

Clover turned to peer at the tribeswoman sitting next to her, and the old lady nodded her head.

"By all means," she said. "We enjoy sharing our gifts without any shame. I don't see why you shouldn't do the same."

Clover glanced at the elder tribespeople playing with themselves while they watched the others performing in the ring, then she pulled off her bodysuit, folding it on the sandy earth under her butt. Then she folded her knees and crossed her legs, slipping her fingers over her wet pussy, groaning softly.

Meanwhile, the woman in the middle of the ring began dancing around the two men standing back-to-back with their erect cocks turned up in the air, pausing every now and then to slide their forked erections between her three orbs, tit-fucking them slowly while they dribbled dew down the front of her glistening stomach.

"Ah," Tara nodded, jilling herself harder while she watched the sexy threesome. "I see there's *another* purpose for those three tits."

"Yeah," Clover panted, pinching her clit between the two forefingers of her right hand. "But I still haven't figured out why the women have four *vulvas* on the front of their abdomen–"

"You'll find out soon enough," the old lady sitting next to her said, glancing at the streams of juices dribbling between Clover's parted thighs.

After a few more minutes of teasing the two tribesmen, the woman in the middle of the fire pit pressed them down onto the ground with their hips facing together and their pronged cocks pointing up like a row of reeds. Then she kneeled over the face of one of the men, leaning forward to swipe her hands over the tops of their tools, bumping them together like she was playing some kind of musical instrument.

"Jezos Maria," Tara said, slipping her fingers into her dripping cunt. "Talk about raining men. Can you imagine having that many hard cocks to work with?"

"I wouldn't know what to do with them," Clover chuckled. "I have a hard enough time managing *two* at a time, let alone four..."

"If you need one to keep yourself distracted," Jessop grunted, jerking his cock with both hands while he watched the action in the middle of the ring. "You're welcome to join me on this side of the circle to keep yourself amused."

"Your turn will come soon enough," Clover grinned, noticing Jessop's purple crown leaking more pre-cum than usual. "I wouldn't want to steal any of your energy before you get a chance to screw one of these native girls."

"Don't worry," Jessop groaned. "This rotating display is more than enough to keep me aroused most of the night."

Suddenly, the woman in the middle of the ring leaned forward, gripping each of the men's poles and pointing them into the slits on her stomach, one at a time. When all four where embedded in her pits, she lay down flat over their connected bodies, writhing her torso over their erections, now deeply ensconced in her cavities. While the trio rocked their bodies to the beat of the drum, the rest of the tribespeople chanted loudly, matching the rising pitch and tempo with their voices.

"Holy fuck," Clover hissed, unable to take her eyes off the writhing threesome while she pressed the tips of her fingers hard against her swelling clit. "What I'd do to have one of those inside *my* pussy right now."

The old lady peered between the legs of the two girls,

watching their masturbation technique with some bemusement.

"I notice you seek most of your pleasure on the *outside* of your cavas," she said. "Don't you have any pleasure centers on the inside?"

"Oh yes, definitely," Clover grunted while she tribbed her fingers over the bottom of her mound. "It's just easier to stimulate the primary sensory organ, where our labia meet at the top."

The woman glanced at Clover's pink folds for a moment, then she drifted her hand between Clover's legs, slowly inserting her fingers into her hole. She moved her fingers around for a few seconds then when she found Clover's G-spot bump, she smiled, pressing her digits more firmly against the front edge of her pussy as she expertly caressed her internal gland.

"Unghh," Clover moaned, tilting her hips upward to welcome the woman's intrusion.

"Does it feel good when I touch you there?" the woman said.

"Yes," Clover sighed, rocking her hips to the beat of the drum while the old lady massaged her G-spot to the rising chants of the crowd.

"You seem to know your way around a *pussy*," Clover grunted, darting her eyes between the trio in the middle of the circle and the old lady fingering her slit.

"I've had a fair amount of practice," the woman said, pressing her fingers harder against Clover's swelling bump as her gland began to fill with fluid. "Your pleasure center is closer to the *opening* of your cava than ours, but one pussy is pretty much the same as another..."

"I'm feeling a bit envious of the girl in the middle having *four* of them," Clover moaned, feeling her orgasm building up while the old lady deftly fingered her. "If she has four times as many pleasure centers as me, I can only *imagine* how intense her orgasms must be when she finally climaxes."

"It doesn't look like it will be long now," the woman smiled, circling her fingers more rapidly over Clover's swelling bump as the drummer's beat rose in tempo and the crowd's chanting escalated to a frenzy.

Meanwhile, the trio in the middle of the fire pit began rocking their bodies together while a waterfall of juices cascaded over the sides of the woman's abdomen and the edges of the two men's hips. When the drummer strummed the animal skin loudly one last time, they raised their heads and grunted in synchronized ecstasy, quivering on the sandy ground while the reflection of the nearby fire danced over their glistening skin.

The woman sitting next to Clover seemed to time the movement of her fingers with the rising pleasure of the performers, until Clover finally climaxed hard and jerked her body forward while she gushed her juices all over the woman's hand. With everybody wailing in unison around the perimeter of the concentric circles, it didn't take long for Tara and Jessop to soon after follow suit, experiencing their second and third orgasms of the still young evening.

6

___

When the trio in the middle of the circle left the ring, the other dancers continued circling around the flowers, until Arel entered the ring alone. Clover and Tara peered at one another with a puzzled expression, then he beckoned to the two women, curling his finger in a come-hither fashion as he bounced and pranced next to the fire.

"It seems that he wants *you* to join him in the circle this time," Clover smiled toward Tara.

"Really?" Tara said, wondering if she was allowed to join in the ceremony along with the rest of the native people.

"I don't see why not," the old woman nodded. "I'm sure our people would be intrigued to see how you humans make love when you join together."

Tara paused for a moment, then she glanced at Clover sitting next to her.

"In that case, can I ask my friend to join me?" she said. "After all, he's got two lingum, and it would be a shame to leave one of them to waste–"

"Of course," the woman smiled. "Normally we pair two

men with one woman, so it will be interesting to see a different grouping this time."

Tara stood up and extended her hand toward Clover, then the two girls wove their way into the rotating circle, dancing with the other tribespeople for a period of time before joining Arel in the inner ring. He flared his eyes when he saw the two women's naked bodies up close, then they approached him slowly, grabbing hold of his forked hard-ons and kissing him on the side of his cheek.

"We're not supposed to kiss other tribeswomen," he panted, reaching out to squeeze the two girls' breasts while he rocked his twin cocks in their hands.

"It's a good thing we're not members of the *tribe* then," Tara smiled, lowering herself slowly down his body as she nibbled on the front of his hairy chest and rock-hard abs.

"Let's see how much you enjoy being kissed by two women *at the same time*," Clover grinned, mimicking Tara while she slid her tongue down his abdomen.

"Oh my God," Arel groaned when they placed their mouths over his two erections, swirling their tongues around his dripping crowns. "I've never been sucked by two women before..."

"Having only one pussy sometimes has its advantages," Tara nodded, smiling up at him. "We have to use our *other* parts to keep our partners amused when there's too many cocks available."

"In that case," Arel grunted, rocking his hips harder against Clover's and Tara's faces as the drumbeat slowly accelerated. "I'm glad I came in here alone."

The two girls turned their faces to smile at one another while they bobbed their heads in unison over Arel's big prongs, reaching behind his ass to play with his balls and tickle his butthole.

"You're going to make me climax if you keep doing that," he growled, placing his hands over the back of their heads as his balls started to tighten.

Tara lifted her face off his throbbing pole, wiping his dripping honey from the side of her lips.

"As much as I'd love to feel you coming in my mouth," she said. "I don't want to waste any of your seed before we get a chance to sample it in a *different* way."

Then she peered over at Clover, who had lifted her head off Arel's other tool.

"Would you like to try a different type of double-P this time?" she said to her friend. "It might be kind of fun to rub our bodies together while we're sitting on his dual prongs..."

"You're reading my mind, girl," Clover grinned, pulling Arel down to the sand next to them and pushing him over onto his back. "Do you feel like facing his *chest* or *legs*?"

Tara paused for a moment while she glanced at Arel's prone body.

"He's already seen me up close when I fucked him in the forest earlier today," she said. "Why don't *you* face him this time while he watches my ass pumping over his cock?"

"That'll work," Clover smiled, squatting over Arel's thighs and pointing one of his bobbing organs toward her slit.

Tara twisted around to face her, then she tilted her ass upward for Arel to have a clear view of her dripping vulva and puckered rosebud.

"By the gods of Jupiter," he groaned, hardly believing he was about to be fucked by two pretty white girls at the same time.

Tara and Clover lowered their bodies over his throbbing poles then they pressed their hips together while slapping their tits against one another. As the chanting of the crowd continued to escalate, they ground their mounds together as their mutual juices dripped down over Arel's balls.

"Holy fuck," he grunted, squeezing the back of Tara's ass as she rocked her hips over his throbbing organ. "This is even better than fucking two cavas on one woman..."

"Because you've got two women sitting on top of you, or because you get to watch us from *behind* this time?" Tara said.

"Both," Arel groaned, digging his fingers deeper into the sides of Tara's ass.

"Yeah, well, it feels twice as good for *us* too," Tara grunted, wrapping her arms around Clover's back and kissing her hard on the mouth as they rocked their hips together.

"Are you ready to give him a show that he'll never forget?" Clover panted, pulling Tara closer while the two women mashed their breasts together.

"Absolutely," Tara smiled, feeling herself nearing the tipping point. "Let it rip..."

Clover pressed her thighs against the side of Tara's hips then she peered up toward the moon, howling like a wild animal as she sprayed her juices over Tara's pussy and Arel's raised balls.

"Nnnghh," she grunted, digging her fingernails into Tara's back.

When Tara felt Clover gushing between her thighs, she wrapped her legs behind her friend's back, locking their hips into a tight embrace while she squirted her own juices over Arel's flexing stomach and astonished face. When he saw the two women squirting together while they moaned into each other mouths, he tensed his leg muscles and curled his toes downward, feeling his twin erections pulsing inside their tight pussies.

"Gahhh!" he grunted, squeezing Tara's ass so tightly he left welts on her skin.

"Mmmft," Tara hissed into Clover's mouth when she felt his organ erupting inside her dripping pussy.

The three partners held onto each other tightly while the drummer pounded a continuous rhythm on his drum with the sound of the tribe chanting loudly in the background. When they finally stopped shaking and came down from their climaxes, no one was in a hurry to decouple and make room for the next group in the circle. But there was still one eager spectator who was looking on from the far circle as he gripped his dripping erection tightly with two hands while he panted in tandem with the performers in the middle of the circle. Unbeknownst to Jessop, it would soon be *his* turn to have a special hookup with one of the tribespeople...

7

After a few minutes, Clover, Tara, and Arel departed the inner ring while the rest of the tribespeople continued dancing around the circle, chanting in rhythm with the drumbeat. Soon after, one of the natives entered the ring alone, and Jessop squinted at the strange girl with three breasts, one stomach slit, and a long, curved cock flexing upward while she swayed her hips seductively to the beat.

"Is she going to have sex *alone*?" Jessop said to the old lady while Clover and Tara took up their previous positions sitting next to her.

"It would appear that way," the woman smiled. "Unless you'd like to join her. Aren't you getting tired of stimulating yourself while your friends are having all the fun?"

"I'd love to get in on the action," he nodded, staring at the sexy hermaphrodite in the middle of the circle. "But I'm not sure where this one would put her cock if I'm the only one making use of her hole..."

"I'm sure the two of you will figure it out," the lady

smiled, noticing the native girl staring at Jessop from the middle of the fire pit.

"Go ahead, Jess," Clover said, watching Jessop's erection bouncing and leaking between his legs. "There's lots of ways I can think of for the two of you to hook up."

"But don't forget to take off your *pants* before you enter the ring," Tara chuckled. "These native people seem to have an aversion to dressing up, and I have a feeling that pretty girl will want to see everything you have to offer."

"Okay," Jessop said, standing up and pulling off his clothes. "But don't you think she'll find me a little...*inadequate*? After all, she's hung a lot better than I am."

"You've got more than enough to satisfy most women," Tara smiled, staring at his eight-inch-long hard-on. "And plenty of *other* equipment to keep her amused."

Jessop peered at his friends with a confused expression, then he joined the rotating ring of dancing tribespeople while they bumped their forked penises and bouncing tits against his back. By the time he entered the ring, he was already dripping in excitement as he stared at the pretty ladyboy with her big, swinging dick. He approached her slowly and when he got close enough, she swiped her pole against his, playfully jousting with him while she swung her three tits teasingly in his direction.

Jessop couldn't resist touching them, and while he pinched her long nipples, she pressed her hips next to his, rubbing their upturned cocks together while she squeezed them with both hands. Jessop groaned as he rocked his hips against hers, frotting their tools together, then he bent down, lowering his face between her three breasts, sucking on her thick bullets and squeezing each of her orbs one at a time.

"He seems to be enjoying himself," Clover smiled,

absent-mindedly fondling Tara's dripping pussy while the two girls watched the action in the inner ring.

"Yes," Tara chuckled. "He looks like a kid in a *candy store.*"

"That's some pretty sweet candy, to be sure," Clover grunted as Tara slipped her fingers inside her swelling slit. "I wouldn't mind a piece of that before the night is over, myself."

"Let's see how things unfold," Tara nodded. "These tribespeople seem to be open to trying just about anything."

"My mind's already wandering with the possibilities," Clover smiled as she watched Jessop and the trans girl exploring each other's bodies.

After a few more minutes of rocking their hips together, the native girl pointed the tip of Jessop's cock toward the dripping slit in the place her navel would normally be, and the look on Jessop's face turned to one of divine ecstasy as he sunk his hard-on into her cavity. The trans girl grabbed his buttocks, sliding her dick between his thighs, then she reached down and angled her hips upward, disappearing her organ between his legs while the two lovers pressed their lips together.

"Is she doing what I *think* she's doing?" Tara said, squinting at the hermaphrodite flexing her hips upward.

"I think so," Clover nodded. "And that's hot as fuck. I wondered if she'd find somewhere else to put that big poker once Jessop found her hole."

"He doesn't seem to be *bothered* by it," Tara panted, rocking her hips to the drumbeat as her friend fingered her pussy.

"On the contrary," Clover chuckled, dripping her own juices over Tara's tribbing fingers. "He seems to be enjoying all the tools at his disposal."

Clover turned to the old lady sitting next to her, noticing

her fingers embedded in her stomach cavity while she watched the couple in the ring.

"Are you okay with them *kissing*?" she said, watching her hand dipping deeper into her dripping cava.

"In this case, there's not so much to worry about," the old lady nodded as a flush began to roll over her face. "She's already self-sufficient in spreading her seed, so if she develops an attraction for another man, that will result in all the more diversity in the offspring she produces."

"You're not worried about our human genes diluting your people's *gifts*?"

"I'm not even sure the mixing would be able to produce a successful conception," the lady said, bouncing her breasts while she fingered each of her slits softly with both of her hands. "We've never tried this before."

"Perhaps it's just as well," Tara chuckled, spreading her legs wider apart as her pleasure began to mount with the increasing pace of the drumbeat. "I'm not sure I'm ready to give birth to a boy with two dicks."

"Or a girl with three *tits*," Clover nodded, humping her hips harder against Tara's hand.

"Either way," Tara grinned, watching Jessop squeezing his buttocks tighter while he sunk his dick deeper into the ladyboy's stomach cavity. "It appears there's going to be a lot of semen exchanging both ways."

While the drummer slowly escalated his tempo toward another crescendo, the two partners in the middle of the pit humped their bodies together while they tongue-fucked each other and gripped each other's bodies tightly.

"Fuck, that's hot," Clover grunted, flexing her body unconsciously forward as she prepared to come all over Tara's trilling hands. "I can't hold it any longer–"

"Me neither," Tara said as Clover pressed her hand deep inside her dripping pussy.

"Neither can I," the old lady groaned, dripping a river of liquid down the front of her stomach while she massaged the inside of her multiple slits.

When the drummer pounded his instruments one last time, Jessop and the ladyboy arched their bodies together, holding onto each other tightly while they groaned in each other's mouths and the rest of the onlooking tribespeople quivered in simultaneous ecstasy, fingering and jerking themselves in obvious delight. When Clover and Tara sprayed their juices between their legs, the old lady next to them grunted in unison, squirting her own juices in a cascade down the middle of her stomach and between her shaking legs. As old as she may have been, there was something incredibly erotic about watching one of the females climaxing with the rest of the group, and Clover's mind began to turn to the *next* potential pairing inside the inner ring...

8

———

When Jessop stumbled out of the ring back toward his friends sitting near the back of the group, he sat down gingerly over his pants lying on the ground, adjusting his semi-tumescent dick while he propped his tired arms behind his ass.

"So did she eventually find somewhere to insert her big dick besides her own hole?" Clover smiled, noticing the flush on his cheeks.

"Yeah," Jessop groaned, adjusting his ass uncomfortably on the hard ground. "I don't know who was deeper inside who, but that was the first time I've ever been fucked up the ass by a *girl*."

"And the first time you fucked one with three *tits*," Tara chuckled.

"That was crazy," Jessop nodded. "It felt weird to be sticking my dick somewhere other than between a woman's legs."

"Did it feel pretty much the same as a normal pussy?" Tara said.

"A little tighter and juicier than most, maybe," Jessop nodded. "But a lot easier to fuck in a *standing* position."

"Something tells me she felt the same way," Tara laughed. "You guys seemed to fit together like two piggies in a blanket."

Jessop glanced between the two girls' legs, noticing their dripping stomachs and inner thighs.

"It looks like you had almost as much fun as I did," he said. "I can't imagine how we're going to top that experience."

"I don't know," Clover grinned. "We still haven't seen *four* people in the ring together–"

"What were you thinking?" the old lady said while she spread her slippery juices over the front of her belly.

"I'd kind of like to see how two *women* enjoy sex together," Clover said. "You mentioned they have some unique ways of stimulating themselves..."

"They do, indeed," the woman said, motioning toward the group dancing around the circle while the drummer picked up his pace. A few spectators handed two of the younger women a pair of cucumbers, and they entered the ring, shaking their hips seductively while they slid the long tubers through the crevasses in their bouncing tits.

"Oh my God," Clover grunted, widening her eyes in excitement. "That's one of my biggest fantasies. I've been dreaming about this match-up all day."

"Would you two like to *join* them?" the lady smiled. "I'm sure they'd enjoy experiencing what human girls feel like just as much as the men. You seem to have some comfort connecting together already..."

"No way," Tara gasped. "We're allowed to fuck them with home-made *dildos*?"

"Or they, *you*," the old lady laughed. "Whichever works

out better for the four of you. Like you said earlier, the possibilities are almost endless."

"What are you waiting for?" Clover said, rising up and this time pulling Tara to her feet. "Let's go do some four-way tribbing. I'm wet enough to fuck a tree trunk. Those cucumbers are looking mighty tasty right about now."

The two girls skipped across the two outer circles, not even bothering to stop and dance with the bouncing group around the inner ring, then they joined the two women caressing one another next to the fire. When they pressed their four bodies together, at first each of the girls was interested in groping their unique body parts, sliding their bellies against one another while they slapped their tits and hips together. When their fingers inevitably found each other's dripping slits, they lay down on the ground, turning face-up and hip-to-hip to keep the sand from falling into their crevasses. Clover and Tara kneeled over the two tribeswomens' faces to give them a clear view of their pussies and the two native girls raised their heads, sticking their faces into their dripping slits while slurping up their juices and circling their tongues over their swollen glands.

"Fuck me," Clover panted, glancing at Tara who was facing her and humping the other girl's face as they both played with the womens' three breasts and elongated nipples. "These native girls sure know how to eat *pussy* for someone who's never seen a human before."

"No kidding," Tara grunted, rocking her hips over her partner's face. "They're better at finding our sweet spots than most men."

"Talking about *sweet spots*," Clover said, peering down at the tribeswomen's bobbing breasts and thick nipples. "Are you thinking the same thing I am?"

"If you're talking about sitting on something a little

bigger and harder than their *faces*, then I'm way ahead of you," Tara nodded, sliding her hands forward over her partner's slippery tits.

"Let's do it," Clover nodded excitedly. "This is something we'll be able to tell our grandkids about some day."

"Yeah, especially if some of them turn out to be *gifted*," Tara chuckled, shifting her hips forward onto her partner's heaving chest.

The two friends placed their dripping pussies over the other girls' breasts, sliding their slippery vulvas back and forth over their three tits while they moaned in pleasure, then they paused their writhing when they felt one of the long nipples entering each of their holes.

"Holy fuck," Tara hissed. "Their nipples are almost as big as a man's *dick*. This is insane!"

"I know," Clover grunted. "The combination of their three breasts sliding over my ass and their big teats stimulating my G-spot is incredible. I could hump their bellies all day..."

"But what about *them*?" Tara said, glancing down at the native girls' pulsing slits dripping copious amounts of lubrication down the sides of their stomachs while the two friends rocked their hips atop their chests. "Shouldn't we be attending to their needs also?"

"I've got a *different* idea how we can stimulate them once we're finished here," Clover huffed, watching the other girls stimulating their holes with the long cucumbers while the two friends fucked their tits. "I just want to see what it feels like to come over their melons before we give them a proper fucking."

"It won't take long for me," Tara grunted, reaching out her arms toward Clover. "Hold my hands while we watch

each other spraying our juices over their pretty stomachs.
I'm almost there–"

Clover interlaced her fingers with Tara's, then she
squeezed her hands tighter as the drummer's tempo began
to speed up, scrunching her face into a tortured expression
until she jerked her hips hard against the native girl's tits,
spraying her juices over her heaving belly while Tara
squealed in simultaneous pleasure, quivering her hips over
her partner's erect nipple.

"Holy fuck!" Tara said when they began to slow the
movement of their hips and loosen their grip on one another's hands. "*That's* something I've never tried before. It was
even hotter than I imagined it."

"Yeah," Clover panted, placing her hands on her partner's slippery belly while she watched the native girl contin-
uing to stimulate herself with the oversize cucumber. "But
I'll tell you what would be even hotter than that. Fucking
these girls with something even *bigger* stuck up our pussies.
Are you ready for a little double-dildo action?"

"Are you *kidding* me?" Tara smiled at her friend. "It's
pretty much all I've been able to think about since the two of
us shared a *different* set of twin phalluses earlier this
evening..."

9

Clover and Tara slid their hips forward a few more inches until they rubbed up against the long cucumbers the native girls had placed inside their cavas, then they raised up and inserted the free ends into their sopping pussies. They could see the other holes in the girls' abdomens between their bodies facing one another, and it was impossible to resist touching them and feeling the juices dribbling out of their slits.

"Mmm, it tastes *sweet*, like the syrup of the yacon tree," Tara said, lifting her dripping fingers to her mouth.

"Yes," Clover nodded, licking the slippery liquid on her fingers. "They appear to lubricate just like us."

"I wonder if they *squirt*, too?" Tara said, circling her fingers around the opening of one of the girl's slits.

"I noticed the old lady did when she climaxed earlier," Clover said. "Maybe it's meant to facilitate the movement of the men's sperm toward their ovaries..."

"Or maybe they jet it out of their openings when their cavas pulse during *orgasm*," Tara smiled, rocking her body up and down on the big cucumber connecting the two partners.

"I dunno," Clover panted, twisting the firm cucumber while she humped her partner's stomach. "But I guarantee there's going to be a lot of fluid coming out soon enough."

Suddenly, the native girl she was sitting on reached around the back of her chest, fondling Clover's breasts. She peered over her shoulder, noticing the girl's flushed face and her three breasts shaking in harmony with the movement of her hips, then she reached back, twisting her big teats like a radio dial.

"Can you believe we're doing this?" Tara huffed, pressing her hand deeper into her partner's hole while she fucked her with the other cucumber. "This is the craziest thing I've ever done–"

"Crazier than fucking a *toadstool* in the forest?" Clover smiled, feeling her pleasure beginning to mount as the drummer accelerated the pace of his pounding.

"Well, at least these girls look like real *people*. And they're a lot prettier than a toadstool."

"Yeah," Clover groaned, peering over Tara's undulating shoulder at the face of her partner who was staring back at her with an expression of delirious pleasure.

"Do you think they climax separately from each hole?" Tara said, twisting her hand deep inside the native girl's free cava. "Let's give them an orgasm like they've never experienced before..."

"Reading my mind," Clover nodded, shifting both of her hands to the stomach of her partner and circling her fingers around the openings of her other slits.

The native girl underneath her grunted in pleasure, and Clover smiled toward Tara, signaling that they should continue.

"They seem to like it," she smiled. "I guess the more, the merrier."

"I'm not quite sure where to stimulate them exactly," Tara said, wrinkling her forehead as she fingered her prone partner.

"The old woman said their pleasure centers are closer to the *ends* of their cavas rather than at the openings, like ours. Maybe if we insert our fingers a little deeper–"

"Yes," Tara nodded, pressing her fingers further inside the native girl's cavity. "I can feel a little bump near the end."

Her partner groaned louder and Clover smiled.

"It looks like you found the sweet spot," she said, pressing her right hand deeper into one of the other girl's holes and caressing the swelling at the end of her tunnel while the native girl grunted and rolled her body harder.

"If two feels better than one," Tara nodded, slipping her other hand into her partner's second opening positioned between the cucumber and Clover's facing body. "We might as well use *both* hands to give them the most pleasure we can."

"Mmm," Clover nodded, slipping her left hand into her partner's other opening. "I've never fingered two pussies at the same time..."

"At least not on the same woman," Tara chuckled, pushing her other hand wrist-deep into the native girl's second cavity.

"I only wish I had more than two hands," Clover said, fisting her partner gently while she teased the swelling at the end of her cavities.

"I only wish I had more than one *pussy*," Tara smiled, pumping her partner's holes with her hands while she rode atop the cucumber deeply embedded in the native girl's third hole.

"I don't know how they do it," Clover panted as she gazed down at the native girls' undulating stomachs and dripping slits. "I'd *faint* if I came from four pussies at the same time."

"It's too bad their fourth one is under our *asses*," Tara grunted, sliding her butt cheeks over the last hole closest to her partner's face.

"Yes," Clover shuddered as she listened to the sound of the two native girls' moans rising in volume. "If there's such a thing as reincarnation, I want to come back as one of these native women."

Tara glanced over at the rotating band of dancers, noticing the hermaphrodite who'd paired up with Jessop earlier staring at the foursome writhing on the ground in front of the raging fire.

"What about as one of those *ladyboys*?" she said, winking at the sexy trans girl. "That could be kind of fun too. You could alternate playing the male and female roles at your leisure."

"Or I could just strap on one of these big cucumbers if I wanted to give them a proper fucking," Clover grunted, feeling her orgasm beginning to well up inside her.

Just as the two friends approached their tipping point, the pretty ladyboy and Jessop suddenly appeared at their side, swinging their dicks in the girls' faces, dancing alongside them with the rest of the frenzied tribespeople chanting at the edge of the circle.

"You're just in time," Clover smiled, peering up at the two interlopers. "Why don't you put those tools to good use and kneel behind our asses while you fuck these girls' last free holes? I think they're almost as close to coming as we are."

"Fuck yes," Jessop said, glancing down at the native girls' three tits bouncing to the beat of the drum and his friends' asses rolling over their spasming slits.

He and the ladyboy knelt over the prone girls' chests, then they angled their hard-ons into the crease behind Clover's and Tara's asses, slowly inserting them deep into the dripping cavas. The two native girls groaned louder, then Jessop and the trans girl wrapped their arms around Clover and Tara's back, squeezing their tits while they pulled themselves closer to their bodies, sinking their dicks all the way into the native girls' leaking holes.

"Oh my God," Jessop grunted, feeling the girl underneath him grab hold of his balls and squeeze them tightly. "Just when I thought this couldn't get any better..."

"That makes *six* of us," Clover grunted, staring into the eyes of the ladyboy who looked like she'd died and gone to heaven from the look of utter bliss on her face.

While the drumbeat inexorably rose in pitch and volume, the tribespeople around the outer circles chanted louder and faster, jilling and jerking themselves while they watched the spectacle in the middle of the ring.

"Holy shit," Clover hissed, feeling Jessop's slippery pole sliding between the crack of her ass. "This is going to be the biggest orgasm I've had in a long time–"

"Yeah," Tara huffed, rolling her eyes back in her head. "Get ready for a lot of juices flying everywhere..."

When she felt the dam burst, Clover squeezed her knees tightly against her partner's stomach, spraying her juices over the native girl's belly, Tara's twitching twat, and Jessop's tightening balls. Seconds later, Tara jerked her body forward, squirting over the ladyboy's pumping dick, then the four holes on the two prone girls' stomachs started spraying up like a giant water fountain, squirting their combined juices over Clover and Tara's faces as they leaned forward to kiss and moan in each other's mouths. While everybody shook their bodies next to the raging fire, the rest of the dancing tribespeople slowly entered the ring, joining together in a jumble of writhing bodies on the sandy court-yard like a nest of mating snakes.

"It's a good thing I didn't let you fire that arrow when you saw the tribesmen surprise us at the edge of the forest," Clover smiled while she blinked her eyes at Tara's flushed face, still dripping from their combined juices.

"Yeah," Tara panted. "It turns out they had a few *more* surprises in store for us..."

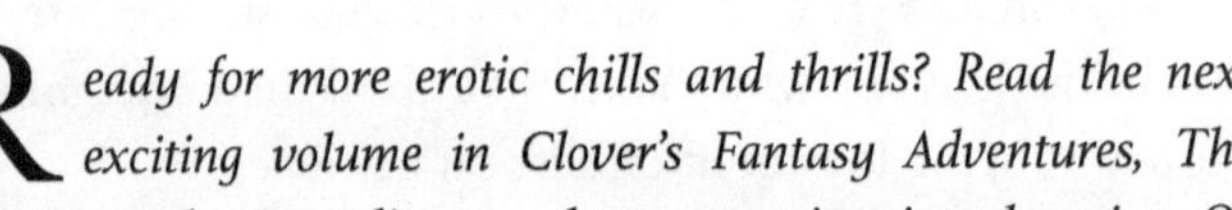

Ready for more erotic chills and thrills? Read the next exciting volume in Clover's Fantasy Adventures, *The Erotic Temple. Buy direct and save at victoriarusherotica. Or download from your favorite online bookstore here: retailer links.*

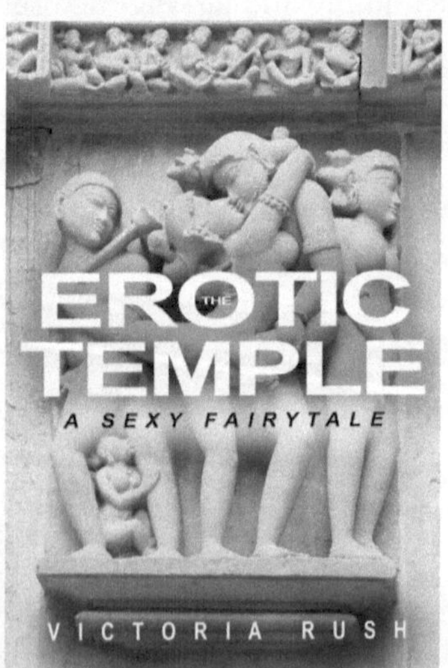

Sometimes a hard man is good to find...

ALSO BY VICTORIA RUSH

Adult Fairytales:

The Enchanted Forest: An Erotic Fairytale

The Land of Giants: An Erotic Fairytale

The Dragon's Lair: An Erotic Fairytale

Witch's Brew: An Erotic Fairytale

The Mage's Spell: An Erotic Fairytale

The Mermaid Lagoon: An Erotic Fairytale

The Coven: An Erotic Fairytale

Rapunzel: An Erotic Fairytale

The Seven Dwarfs: An Erotic Fairytale

The Land of Mutants: An Erotic Fairytale

The Erotic Temple: A Sexy Fairytale (Coming Soon)

Erotica Themed Bundles:

Voyeur: Lesbian Erotica Bundle

Public Affairs: A Lesbian Anthology

Futa Fantasies: The Ladyboy Collection

Threesomes: The Lesbian Collection

Threesomes - Volume 2: The Lesbian Collection

First Time: A Lesbian Anthology

Hedonism: An Erotic Anthology

Switch Hitters: Bisexual Erotica

Taboo Erotica: The Lesbian Series

BDSM: The Lesbian Collection

Party Games: The Erotic Collection

Party Games 2: The Erotic Collection

All Girl 1: Lesbian Erotica Bundle

All Girl 2: Lesbian Erotica Bundle

All Girl 3: Lesbian Erotica Bundle

All Girl 4: Lesbian Erotica Bundle

Erotic Fairytale Bundles:

Clover's Fantasy Adventures: Books 1 - 5

Clover's Fantasy Adventures: Books 6 - 10

Erotic Fantasy:

Pirate's Bounty: A Time Travel Adventure

Wild West: A Time Travel Adventure

Private Riley: A Time Travel Adventure

Cleopatra's Secret: A Time Travel Adventure

Bounty Hunter 2125: A Time Travel Adventure

Ninja Assassin: A Time Travel Adventure

The 300: A Time Travel Adventure

Arabian Nights: An Erotic Fairytale (coming soon…)

Steamy Time Travel Bundles:

Riley's Time Travel Adventures: Books 1 - 5

Lesbian Erotica:

The Dinner Party: Lesbian Voyeur Erotica

The Darkroom: Bisexual Voyeur Erotica

Naked Yoga: Lesbian Transgender Erotica

Nude Cruise: Bisexual Voyeur Erotica

Rush Hour: Taboo Public Sex

The Girl Next Door: First Time Lesbian Erotic Romance

Girls' Camp: Lesbian Group Sex

Wet Dream: Ladyboy Fantasy Erotica

The Convent: Taboo Sex with a Nun

Sex Robot: A Dream Sex Machine

The Personal Trainer: Getting Pumped at the Gym

The Dominatrix: BDSM Lesbian Domination

Webcam Chat: Lesbian Online Sex

Paint Me: A Kinky Bodypainting Workshop

The Toy Party: Girls Sharing Sex Toys

The Costume Party: Strapping One On

Swedish Sauna: Lesbian Group Sex

The Therapist: Taboo Lesbian Erotica

Elevator Shaft: Bisexual Threesomes Erotica

Ladyboy: Lesbian Transgender Erotica

Peep Show: Lesbian Voyeur Erotica

The Dare: Public Sex Erotica

Maid Service: Lesbian Threesomes Erotica

The Hitchhiker: First Time Lesbian Erotica

The Housesitter: Spycam Lesbian Erotica

The Spa: Lesbian Group Orgy

Parlor Games: Blindfold Sex Party

The Exchange Student: First Time Lesbian Erotica

The Hostel: Bisexual Group Erotica

The Harem: Lesbian Erotic Romance

The Orient Express: Lesbian Voyeur Erotica

The First Lady: A Forbidden Lesbian Erotic Romance

The Slave: Lesbian BDSM Erotica

The Masseuse: Lesbian Sensuous Erotica

Too Close for Comfort: Lesbian Forbidden Erotica

Naked Twister: A Wild Party Game

Lexi: The Sex App (Lesbian Fantasy Erotica)

Call Girl: Lesbian Bisexual Threesomes Erotica

Circle Jill: Lesbian Masturbation Workshop

The Viewing Room: Masturbation Voyeur Erotica

Spin the Bottle: A Kinky Party Game

The Hair Salon: Lesbian Voyeur Erotica

Tribadism 1: Girls Only Sex Workshop

Tribadism 2: The Art of Scissoring

Tribadism 3: Threeway Hookups

The Kiss: A Game of Oral Sex

Pledge Week: Sorority Sisters

Carny Games 1: A Wild Sex Party

Carny Games 2: A Kinky Sex Party

Carny Games 3: An Erotic Sex Party

Dreamscape: An Artificial Reality Game

Glory Hole: Guess Who's On the Other Side

Joy Ride: A Late Night Erotic Bus Trip

The Blind Girl: An Erotic Romance(Coming Soon)

Lesbian Erotica Bundles:

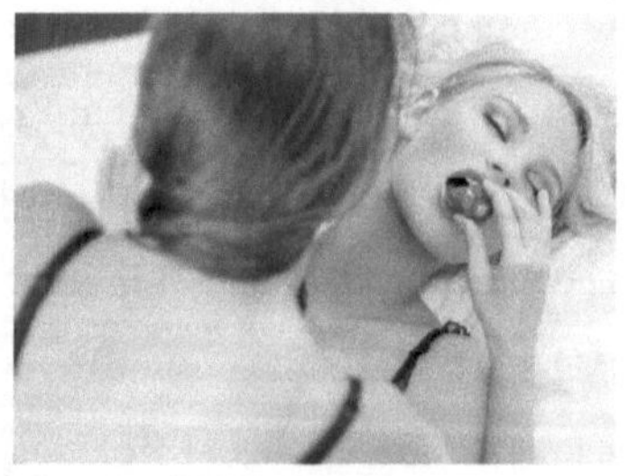

Jade's Erotic Adventures: Books 1 - 5

Jade's Erotic Adventures: Books 6 - 10

Jade's Erotic Adventures: Books 11 - 15

Jade's Erotic Adventures: Books 16 - 20

Jade's Erotic Adventures: Books 21 - 25

Jade's Erotic Adventures: Books 26 - 30

Jade's Erotic Adventures: Books 31 - 35

Jade's Erotic Adventures: Books 36 - 40

Jade's Erotic Adventures: Books 41 - 45

Jade's Erotic Adventures: Books 46 - 50

Fifty Shades of Jade: Superbundle

Standalone Stories:

The Polynesian Girl: A Lesbian EroticRomance

FOLLOW VICTORIA RUSH:

Want to keep informed of my latest erotic book releases? Sign up for my newsletter and receive a FREE bonus book:

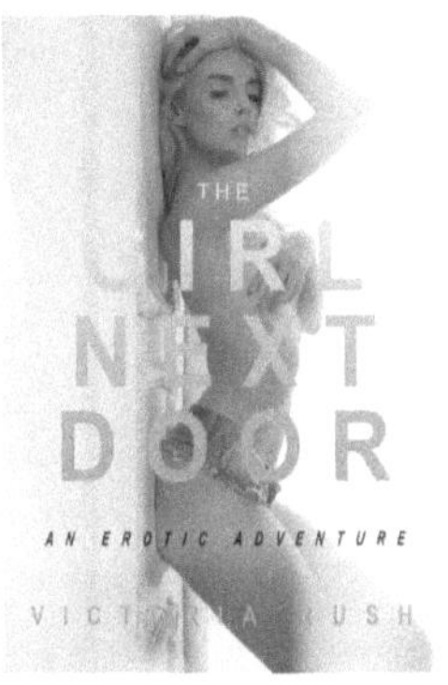

Spying on the neighbors just got a lot more interesting...

www.ingramcontent.com/pod-product-compliance
Lightning Source LLC
Chambersburg PA
CBHW061552310726
48972CB00008B/2722